Thomas' Busy Day

The Rev. W. Awdry

Every morning, Thomas wakes up bright and early in the engine shed. When his Driver has stoked up his boiler, he is ready for another busy day.

First stop is the station platform.
Thomas' passengers wait for him to take them
to the town.

The Fat Controller makes sure he leaves on time.

When he reaches the town, Thomas' passengers go to work. New passengers climb aboard and he takes them to the harbour.

At the harbour, Thomas drops off his passengers. There is a lot of work to do, but Thomas takes time to talk to Percy.

Once his afternoon's work at the docks is finished, it is time to travel back to The Fat Controller's station.

Finally it is time to return to the engine shed.
The other engines are already back from their
journeys.

It has been a busy day for the engines and soon they are all asleep. Good night, Thomas!

James'
Difficult Day

The Rev. W. Awdry

It is a lovely sunny morning and James can't wait to start the day.
But poor James does not know what a difficult day he will have.

Not long after James begins his journey,
his brakes catch fire! Flames and sparks stream
from his wheels.

"Help! Help!" shouts James, as he crashes through the hedge into a field.

Poor James has to wait a long time
to be rescued.
The breakdown train lifts him
back on to the track where the
workmen repair his brakes.

At last, James sets off to the station.
The Fat Controller has heard all about
James' accident.
"Take the rest of the day off, James," he says.
"You deserve it after such a difficult day."

That evening, back at the engine shed, James tells the other engines about his adventure.

As they all fall asleep, James hopes that
tomorrow will be a better day.
Good night, James!